Sparkle: A Star's Story

Kristina Warden

an imprint of

WINDMILL
BOOKS ™
New York

Published in 2009 by Windmill Books, LLC
303 Park Avenue South, Suite # 1280, New York, NY 10010-3657

First Edition

Book Design and Illustrations by: Planman Technologies (India) Pvt. Ltd.

Publisher Cataloging Data

Warden, Kristina
        Sparkle : a star's story / by Kristina Warden.
p.   cm. – (Nature stories)
Summary: Sparkle tells how stars are formed and introduces some of her family,
including Sally and Sam, who are protostars; Uncle Al, a red giant; Aunt Annie, a supernova; and Grandpa Herbert, a white dwarf.
ISBN 978-1-60754-086-1 (lib.) – ISBN 978-1-60754-087-8 (pbk.)
ISBN 978-1-60754-088-5 (6-pack)
        1. Stars—Juvenile fiction   [1. Stars—Fiction]   I. Title   II. Series
        [E]—dc22

Manufactured in the United States of America

My name is Sparkle. If you look out your bedroom window at night, you might be able to see me. I don't like to brag, but the fact is—I'm a STAR!

My aunt's pretty cool, too. Well, actually, she's very hot! She has the brightest orange hair you've ever seen. In fact, my aunt is bright all over. You need sunglasses to look at her, so you don't hurt your eyes. If you haven't guessed yet, my aunt is the Sun. She's a star, too!

I have millions of brothers and sisters and cousins. There are so many of us that we fill the night sky. We're there during the day, too, but you can't see us because the sky is too bright. That's my aunt's time to shine.

6

You probably don't remember the day you were born, do you? I don't remember the day I was born either. All I know is that I was in a big cloud of dust and gas all clumped together. More and more matter kept clumping together in my part of the cloud, and pretty soon I was a protostar. That's what a baby star is called.

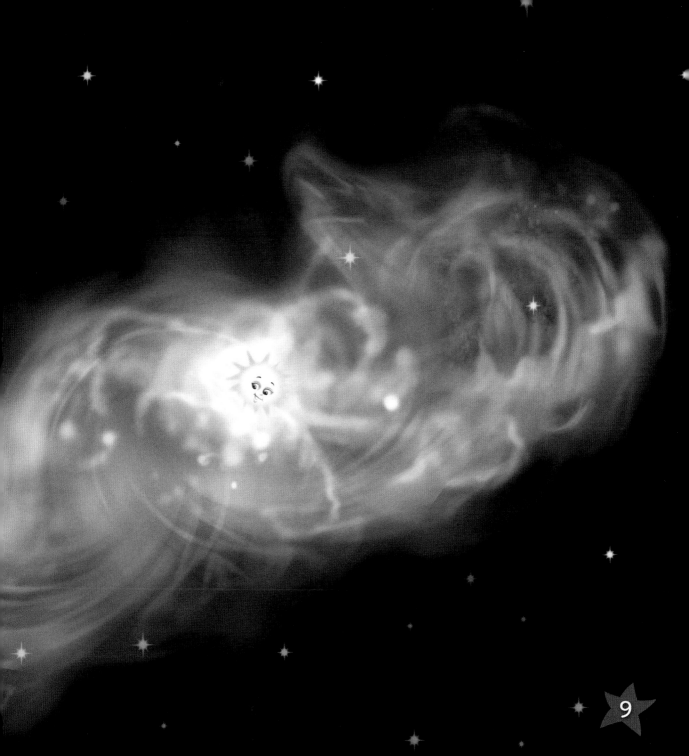

When I was just a protostar I spent a lot of time growing. It's hard work for a star to grow up. It takes a lot of heat and energy. But I kept at it, so I could be full of hot air just like my big brother!

11

Now that I'm getting bigger, I have some important jobs, like sending light toward Earth, where you live! It's neat that we are so far apart, but we can still see each other.

13

It looks pretty fun down where you are, but I have a lot of fun up here, too. My family's out of this world.

My little brother and sister, Sally and Sam, as protostars

Uncle Al: He's a red giant

Aunt Annie: She's a Supernova and Uncle Al says she has an explosive temper!

Grandpa Herbert is a White Dwarf, but he's always complaining about getting stuck in a black hole

I like exploring the sky, but I make sure to stay on a path, like all stars do. I always make sure I can see my aunt, the Sun, so I don't get lost. Each day I use my energy to send light and heat into space. That's my day job *and* my night job!

17

At bedtime, I shine as bright as I can to help light up the night sky. In fact, I'm my own nightlight. I can be *your* nightlight too.

18

19

When stars get really old—and I mean billions of years old—they implode. It's a pretty exciting explosion. Some of the stardust from the explosion scatters in outer space and helps make new stars. But *I* still have a lot of shining to do, and I bet you do, too!

21

So don't forget to wave to me when you look out your bedroom window at night. Even though I'm up here in space and you're down there on Earth, we have a lot in common. I bet you're a star in your family, just like I am in mine!

23

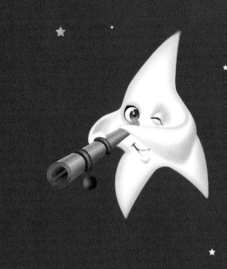

For more great fiction and nonfiction,
go to windmillbooks.com.